One Little Angel

Once upon a time, long, long ago,
a huge, bright star appeared in the sky.
It was there to tell the world about
the birth of a very important baby.
Everyone, from the humblest shepherd
to the wisest of wise men, wanted
to go and greet the newborn child.
Everyone, that is, except . . .

For Rose and Molly Syrett

A Red Fox Book

Published by Random House Children's Books
20 Vauxhall Bridge Road, London SW1V 2SA

A division of The Random House Group Ltd
London Melbourne Sydney Auckland
Johannesburg and agencies throughout the world

3 5 7 9 10 8 6 4

First published in Great Britain by Andersen Press Ltd 1998
Red Fox edition 2000

Printed in Hong Kong by Midas Printing Ltd

THE RANDOM HOUSE GROUP Limited Reg. No. 954009
www.randomhouse.co.uk

ISBN 0-09-940436-2

One Little Angel

Ruth Brown

RED FOX

"I'M NOT GOING!" said the
little angel, stamping her foot.
The other angels were shocked.

"You've got to go," they whispered. "Gabriel said
we've *all* got to go. He said we had to shine like stars
in the sky and then go down and greet the baby.
Everyone will be there and he'll be
ever so cross if you're not."
"Well, he won't know, will he?"
said the little angel.

"If I stay up here until it's all over and
you don't tell him, then he won't know."
"Yes, he will," chorused the other angels.
"Gabriel knows everything. Don't you remember?
He told us he did. He knows if you tell a lie.
He knows if you poke your tongue out at someone
and he *always* knows if you say rude words.

So he's bound to know if you don't
do what he said. Come on!"

But the little angel would not go with them
and so they left her alone in the dark.
"I don't care," she muttered. "I don't want
everybody staring at me wearing this silly halo
and these stupid wings.

Anyway, I can see everything from up here."
The little angel looked down at the scene below.
Although she didn't want to join in, she definitely
didn't want to miss anything.
She saw the shepherds with their lambs . . .

. . . she saw the three wise men
with their precious gifts
of gold, frankincense and myrrh . . .

. . . she saw the innkeeper and his wife,
the cow, the horse, the donkey and the angels.
She leant forward just a little further
to see them all gathered round, gazing
in silent wonder at the tiny baby.

Suddenly, the darkness just slipped away.

Everyone looked up.
The little angel was bathed in light
from the scene below.

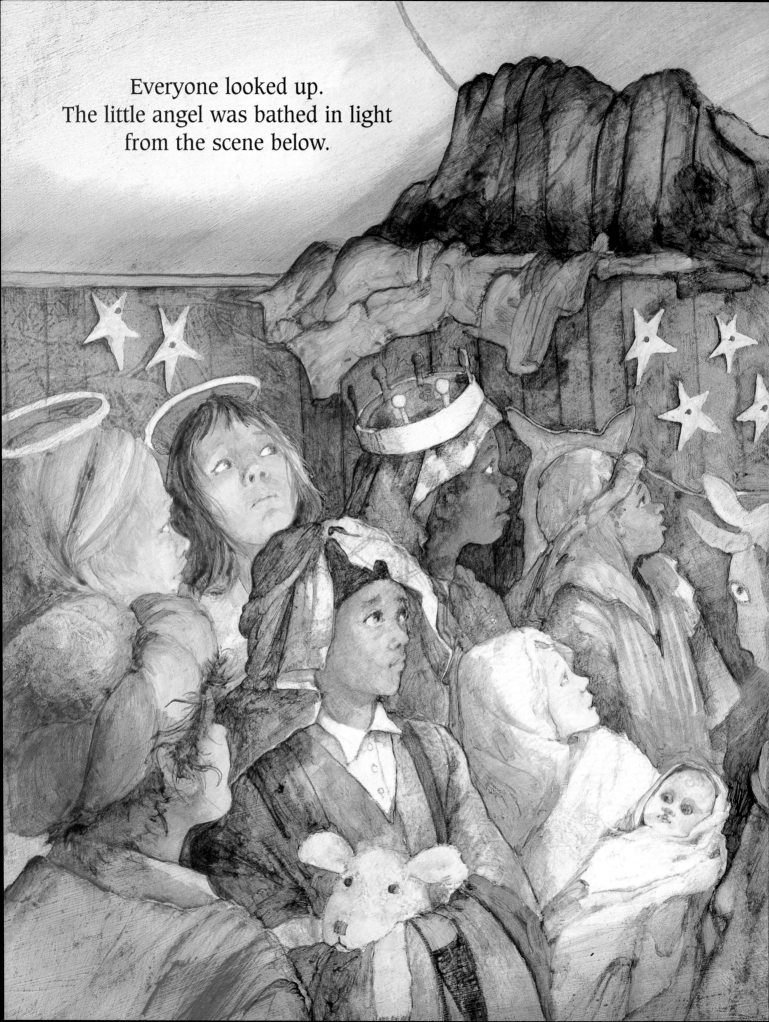

The little angel didn't move.
She *couldn't* move. She was petrified.
But just as her lip began to tremble,
the silence was broken by the sound of loud
applause echoing round the school hall.

The little angel, shining brighter than
the brightest star, smiled —

— and so did everyone else.
Especially the headteacher, Mr Gabriel.

THE END